P9-DVM-887

BATCAT
and the SEVEN SQUIRRELS

CALGARY PUBLIC LIBRARY

JAN - - 2018

CALGARY PUBLIC LIBRARY

JAN -- 2011

BATCAT

and the SEVEN SQUIRRELS

ERIC WALTERS

Illustrated by
KASIA CHARKO

ORCA BOOK PUBLISHERS

Text copyright © 2016 Eric Walters
Illustrations copyright © 2016 Kasia Charko

All rights reserved. No part of this publication may be reproduced or transmitted in
any form or by any means, electronic or mechanical, including photocopying,
recording or by any information storage and retrieval system now known or
to be invented, without permission in writing from the publisher.

Library and Archives Canada Cataloguing in Publication

Walters, Eric, 1957–, author
Batcat and the seven squirrels / Eric Walters ; illustrated by Kasia Charko.
(Orca echoes)

Issued in print and electronic formats.
ISBN 978-1-4598-1255-0 (paperback).—ISBN 978-1-4598-1256-7 (pdf).—
ISBN 978-1-4598-1257-4 (epub)

I. Charko, Kasia, 1949, illustrator II. Title. III. Series: Orca echoes
PS8595.A598B38 2016   jc813'.54   C2016-900532-1
C2016-900533-x

First published in the United States, 2016
Library of Congress Control Number: 2016931876

Summary: In this early chapter book, Nathan learns to care for
seven orphaned baby squirrels with help from a stray neighborhood cat.

Orca Book Publishers gratefully acknowledges the support for its publishing programs
provided by the following agencies: the Government of Canada through the Canada Book Fund
and the Canada Council for the Arts, and the Province of British Columbia
through the BC Arts Council and the Book Publishing Tax Credit.

Cover artwork and interior illustrations by Kasia Charko
Author photo by Sofia Kinachtchouk

ORCA BOOK PUBLISHERS
www.orcabook.com

Printed and bound in Canada.

19 18 17 16 • 4 3 2 1

To Batcat

CHAPTER ONE

Nathan looked up from his meal and out the window. There was something pressed against the screen of the door. It was pinned there, moving as the wind blew it back and forth, back and forth. He thought it was very strange how it was moving. Was it a black plastic bag or a piece of paper or…no, it was furry, and it had a tail, and—

"It's a squirrel!" Nathan yelled as he jumped up from the table.

He ran across the kitchen. His father and mother were right behind him. He skidded to a stop at the thin screen door standing between him and the squirrel. His parents stood beside him.

"It's just a baby," his mother said.

Instead of running away, the little squirrel continued to cling to the screen. It tilted its head to the side and looked in at them as they looked out at it.

"He's so cute," Nathan said.

"He *is* cute, but what's he doing here?" his mother asked.

"Maybe he wants to come in and join us for supper," his father joked.

"Could he?" Nathan asked. "I'd share my salad with him."

"He should go back and join *his* family for dinner," Nathan's mother said. She looked at her husband, and he nodded in agreement.

"Time to go home, little guy," his father said as he gently tapped one of his fingers against the screen.

Instead of running off, the squirrel climbed up the screen until it was at the spot where he'd been tapping. His father moved his finger and tapped at another spot on the screen, and the little animal followed after his finger.

"So what do we do now?" Nathan asked.

"We could close the door, and he might go away," his father suggested.

"That would be rude," Nathan said.

"But it's not like we can bring him in."

Nathan leaned in a little closer to the squirrel. "He's crying."

"I don't think squirrels cry," his mother said. "But I do hear something... it's squeaking."

"He's probably calling for his mother to come and get him," Nathan said.

Nathan's father went to close the door and hesitated. He knew Nathan was concerned. "It'll be okay, Nathan. I'm sure his mother will come and get him as soon as we close the door."

Nathan wanted to believe his father, but he was worried. He nodded his head ever so slightly in agreement.

His father slowly started to close the door and—

"Wait!" Nathan called out. "Look!"

His father stopped. He hoped he'd see the mother squirrel. Instead, he saw what his son had seen.

"It's Batcat," Nathan said.

Batcat was a stray cat that roamed the neighborhood. Nobody owned the cat, so he didn't really have a name. But Nathan had started calling him Batcat because while he was mostly black, the lower half of his face was white. It looked like he was wearing a mask—just like the comic-book character.

"Do cats like squirrels?" Nathan asked.

"Not in the way we'd like," his father said.

The big old cat sat on the fence. He was staring right at them—and at the little squirrel. His tail was swinging ever so slightly. There was a little kink in it where it had been injured at some time. His ears were pressed down. His left ear had a chunk that was missing.

Slowly Nathan's father opened the door. The squirrel clung to the screen as it swung out. His father walked across the deck toward where Batcat sat on the fence.

"You have to leave now," he said to the cat.

Batcat didn't move. This wasn't a cat used to being told what to do by anybody.

"Scat, cat!" Nathan's father said and gestured with his hands.

Batcat's tail swished a little bit harder, and his green eyes blazed angrily. For a second Nathan's father felt a bit uneasy, like he was walking toward a tiger instead of an alley cat. He knew that

was silly, but still, the cat was staring at him so intently. What would he do if the cat didn't leave?

Then, as he got closer, the big tom turned and started walking away, carefully balanced on the top of the fence. He got to the end of the property and then jumped down and disappeared into the next yard.

It was good that the cat was gone, but Nathan's dad felt bad about chasing him away. He'd been secretly feeding the stray without his wife or Nathan knowing. What he didn't realize was that both Nathan and his mother had been doing the same thing. There were lots of people in the neighborhood who were feeding Batcat. This was a cat that was owned by nobody but helped by many.

Nathan opened the door just enough that he could slip out too. The little squirrel suddenly leaped off the screen and landed on his shoulder!

CHAPTER TWO

Nathan almost screamed. His mother did scream. But there was no reason for either of them to be afraid. The squirrel was so little and light that it was like he wasn't even there. He snuggled into Nathan, putting his little head under the collar of his shirt like he was trying to hide or burrow in.

Almost instantly, Nathan's parents were both standing beside him on the deck.

"Are you okay?" his father asked.

"I'm okay."

"Is he dangerous?" his mother asked.

"No, I don't think so," his father answered.

"He's just a baby," Nathan said. "And he's scared. I can feel him shaking."

His mother gently pushed back the collar of her son's shirt to take a closer look. The little squirrel looked up at her, and he did look scared. She felt sad for him—and protective. She was the only mother around right now, and this little guy did need a mother.

"It's all right, little squirrel," she said. "You're in good hands now. We'll take care of you."

"We will?" his father asked.

"What other choice do we have?" she said.

"I've seen a lot of squirrels in the trees here," his father said.

There was a big tree right beside their porch.

"I'm sure if we just put him in the tree, his mother will come back and get him," he added.

"I'm not so sure," Nathan's mother said. She hesitated. "I didn't want to mention it, but there was a squirrel on the road in front of our house a few days ago."

There were always lots of squirrels on the street, so Nathan and his dad knew there had to be more to the story.

"It was dead. It had been run over by a car," she said.

"But that doesn't mean it was the mother of this squirrel," Nathan said.

"I don't know if it was this one's mother, but it was a mother. It was missing most of the fur on its tail."

Nathan knew what that meant. He'd asked his parents about it in the past, when he'd seen a squirrel with almost no fur on its tail. His parents explained how squirrels pulled the fur off their tails to line the nests for their babies. The fur made the nests warm and snuggly.

"So you think this little guy could be an orphan," his father said.

"But what about the father squirrel?" Nathan asked.

"Father squirrels don't help raise the babies. He's long gone, so if the mother is dead…well…"

"Then he'd have nobody," Nathan said.

"That's possible," his mother said.

"So if we just put him in the tree, there won't be anybody to care for him. He could just starve to death," Nathan said.

"Or worse," his father added.

Nathan wondered what could be worse than starving. Then his father pointed to the back of the yard. There, at the far end, was Batcat. He had returned. He was sitting on the fence again, looking at them—well, really, looking at the squirrel on Nathan's shoulder.

"So we can't put him in a tree, and we can't leave him out. What else is left?" his father asked.

"There's only one thing we can do," Nathan said. "He has to come inside with us."

His parents looked at each other like they were trying to figure out what to say.

"I guess there's one other choice," Nathan said.

"There is?" his father asked.

"Yes. If he can't come inside, then I'm going to have to sleep out here."

"You can't sleep outside," his mother said.

"Then I guess there *is* only one choice. So he can come inside when I go inside...right?"

His parents both smiled and nodded their heads in agreement.

Nathan almost cheered out loud but realized that would scare the little guy. And the last thing he wanted to do was scare him any more than he already was.

Just then the little squirrel let him know that he agreed with their decision as he crawled into the pocket of Nathan's shirt.

CHAPTER THREE

The little squirrel lapped up water from the pan.

"He was really thirsty," Nathan said.

"There's no telling how long it's been since he had anything to drink," his father said. "I'm just glad he's been weaned."

Nathan gave him a confused look.

"Squirrels are mammals, and all mammals nurse from their mother.

Because he's been weaned, we know he's older, and that's good."

"It is?" Nathan asked.

"Older means he has a better chance of surviving," his mother explained.

Nathan hadn't even thought that could be a problem. Now he felt worried. "Should we give him milk then?"

"Cow's milk is probably very different from squirrel milk. If he's old enough to drink, water is probably the best thing."

"He must be hungry too. What exactly do squirrels eat?" Nathan asked. "You know, besides peanuts."

His mother had opened up the laptop to google squirrels.

"It does say nuts, seeds, fruits, pinecones, fungi and green vegetables," she said.

"And French fries," Nathan added.

"No, there's nothing here about French fries," she said.

"I guess he doesn't know that," Nathan said.

The squirrel had grabbed a fry off Nathan's plate and was nibbling away at it.

"He's as hungry as he was thirsty," Nathan said.

"He probably hasn't eaten for a while, but still, let's be good parents and give him something a little more squirrelly," his father said.

He had a couple of peanuts that he placed upon the table. The squirrel dropped the fry and picked up one of the peanuts.

"Way to go, Mr. Munch," Nathan said.

"Mr. Munch?" his father said.

"I thought he needed a name. It could be just Munch, or Munchie."

"But only his closest friends should get to call him Munchie," his father said.

"I think we're his only friends," Nathan said. Then he thought of something. "When squirrels have babies, do they just have one?"

"I'm not sure," his father said.

"I'm looking it up," his mother said.

Once again she started googling squirrel information.

"It says that there are generally three to five in a litter," she said.

"So there might be two to four more babies out there, alone, hungry and thirsty," Nathan said.

"There could be," his mother agreed.

"Unless they come to our door, I'm not sure there's much we can do about it," his father said.

"There has to be something," Nathan said.

"Short of climbing up every tree to look for nests, I'm not sure what else we can do," his father said.

"We have a ladder, right?" Nathan asked.

"Yes, we have a ladder, but…" His father stopped himself midsentence. He knew the answer he was going to give wasn't the right answer. "I'll get the ladder."

There were five big trees and several little trees surrounding the yard. While any of those big trees could hold a nest, it made sense to search the one closest to the porch first. Besides, Nathan's mother was sure she'd seen the mother squirrel in that tree more than the others.

Nathan's father stood at the bottom of the ladder, holding it secure while his mother climbed up. She was much more comfortable being high up than he was. She was the one who always put up the Christmas lights and cleaned out the eaves troughs.

She climbed higher and higher, until she almost disappeared into the canopy of leaves and branches.

Nathan, with Munchie sitting on his shoulder, stood just off to the side. Both of them were looking up at his mother.

"Do you see anything?" Nathan yelled.

"I can see that our roof is going to need to be replaced before too long," she called down.

"You know what I mean!" he said.

"Nothing yet...wait."

As they watched from the ground, she climbed off the ladder and onto

a large branch shooting off from the trunk.

"Should you be doing that?" Nathan's father asked.

"I'm fine. Don't worry. The branch is solid, and I'm holding on. Besides, it's the only way I can get to the nest."

"There's a nest! You found the nest!" Nathan yelled.

"She found *a* nest," his father said. "It doesn't mean it belongs to Munchie and his family or that it's even being—"

Nathan's mother made a strange noise. It was a combination of surprise and happiness. Before they could even ask what had happened, she began to laugh.

"Are you all right?" Nathan's father called as he peered up at her.

"I'm fine," she said. "Matter of fact, we're *all* fine."

CHAPTER FOUR

In the end, there were six more baby squirrels. The first four had come out of the nest by themselves and had clung to Nathan's mother's shirt. With the last two, she had gently reached into the nest with her gloved hands and placed them in the pockets of her shirt. Those squirrels were the smallest two.

Now they were all scampering around on the kitchen floor. Seven little patches of grayish red fur and shiny eyes. They kept returning to the pan of water to drink and to nibble from the bowl that was filled with nuts, seeds, berries and cut-up veggies. It was a combination of food from Nathan's house and the bird feed set out for neighborhood birds. They all knew that squirrels seemed to like whatever was in bird feeders.

"They seem okay, right?" Nathan asked.

"They seem really good. I'm just not sure what we do now," his mother said.

"We keep them," Nathan said. "You and Dad promised I could have a pet and—"

"A pet is a dog or a cat. One dog or one cat, not seven dogs or seven cats. Squirrels are wild animals and need to be in the wild."

She could see how worried and upset Nathan looked. She placed an arm around his shoulder. "We can't *keep* them, but we are going to try to *raise* them."

"Really?"

"Really, but it's not going to be easy, and it's going to take a lot of time and a lot of work," she said. "Are you prepared to work hard?"

"I'll work as hard as I can. I promise."

"And with school ending and summer vacation starting for both of us, we'll have time to devote to them," she said.

Nathan's father walked into the room. He was carrying a wooden box. He'd been in the basement, and they had heard him working with power tools, so they knew he was building something.

"Ta-da!" he said as he placed the box on the table. "Here it is."

"What exactly is it?" Nathan's mother asked.

"It's a squirrel hotel. This is the entrance," he said, spinning it around to show them a small opening.

ACORN HOTEL

"And this is the inside." He undid a little latch and the whole top of the box swung open on hinges. The inside was lined with blankets and towels.

"It looks nice and soft," Nathan said. "Do you think they'll like it?"

"There's only one way to find out."

His father closed the lid and then carefully placed the box on the floor among the baby squirrels. At first they didn't seem to notice. Then one of them started sniffing it, and a second got up on his back paws to try to look over it. A third, his cheeks full of seeds, jumped up on top and started eating.

"You're supposed to go inside," Nathan explained to them.

Then, almost like he understood, Munchie peeked inside and then disappeared into the box.

"I think this just might work," his father said.

The squirrel hotel sat in the corner of Nathan's room. All seven squirrels were nestled within. Nathan opened the lid slightly so he and his parents could look inside. The squirrels were all cuddled together in one big ball of fur and tails, surrounded by a pink towel.

"So cute," his mother whispered.

"We better let them sleep," his father said, and Nathan lowered the lid and softly closed it.

"Now that we have seven babies asleep, we have to get the eighth to bed," his father said.

"I'm not a baby," Nathan protested. "I'm almost eight."

"And a very grown-up eight," his father said. "Because now you're like a parent to seven babies."

His father picked up Nathan and carried him to bed. His mother tucked him in. This started their bedtime routine of his parents lying beside him and all three of them reading together. They'd hardly started the story when Nathan's eyelids got heavy, and it looked like he was asleep.

Quietly Nathan's parents got off the bed and turned out the big light, leaving the room with a little glow from the night-light in the corner. As they started to pull the door closed, Nathan called out.

"What will happen with the squirrels tomorrow?" he asked.

"They'll be fine," his mother said.

"Will they?" he asked.

"We'll do the best we can," his father said. "Day by day, we'll do the best we can for them."

CHAPTER FIVE

The squirrels scampered around the backyard as Nathan and his mother sat on the porch. They'd grown so much bigger in the past two weeks.

"You be careful up there, Scruffy!" Nathan called out as the squirrel jumped onto the fence.

"I still don't know how you can tell them all apart," his mother said.

"I still don't know how you and Dad can't. They're all so different."

Scruffy was missing a patch of fur on one side. Fluffy was, well, the fluffiest. Patches had a tiny patch of white fur on his right back leg. Bushy had the thickest, longest tail. Shiny had the brightest eyes, and Rocky had the biggest cheeks.

Nathan had named all of them except Rocky. His father had said it was sort of like a law that if you had seven squirrels, one of them had to be called Rocky. He also said that if they ever had a pet moose, he'd have to be called Bullwinkle. Nathan thought a pet moose would be pretty cool and agreed to the name.

And, of course, there was Munchie. He was the biggest and probably the oldest. They figured that's why he had been strong enough to climb down from the tree by himself to get help.

Nathan, like a good squirrel parent, constantly looked around the yard for anything that could harm them.

"Have you seen Batcat today?" Nathan asked.

"Not today, not yet."

The big cat was often there watching the squirrels when they were out playing in the yard.

"I guess it's my fault that he's around so much," his mother said.

Nathan gave her a questioning look.

"Sometimes I used to feed him," she said.

"Me too," Nathan admitted. "Sometimes I still put scraps out for him in the back of the yard. That's okay, right?"

"It's hard not to like the old guy. You know, he even let me pet him once," said Nathan's mom.

"He lets me pet him too," Nathan said. "Sometimes he even purrs, but it's a strange purr."

"What do you mean?"

"It's all gravelly and bumpy like his purr machine is broken."

"That's not surprising. Between his bent tail and missing part of his ear, I think he's had a pretty hard life."

"He's sort of like our squirrels," Nathan said.

"What do you mean?"

"He's an orphan too. There's nobody to care for him either."

"The squirrels are lucky. They have you," his mother said. She reached over to give Nathan's hand a squeeze, but Nathan suddenly jumped to his feet.

"Munchie, look out!" he screamed.

A white cat was slinking across the grass toward Munchie, whose back was turned so he couldn't see it coming.

Nathan had only run a few steps before the cat leaped into the air—and then there was a bolt of black as the white cat was knocked off to the side! It had been hit by another cat. It was Batcat!

The two cats hissed and screamed and snarled. Then the white cat jumped to its feet and ran away. Batcat chased after it for a few steps and then stopped as it leaped over the fence and was gone.

Munchie was safe. Or was he?

The little squirrel was bouncing across the lawn, right toward Batcat! The cat turned and sat down, and the little squirrel snuggled into him. Batcat raised a front paw and placed it on the back of the squirrel. He then leaned over and started licking the squirrel.

Nathan couldn't believe his eyes. Neither could his mother. Slowly the two of them inched forward until they were crouched above the two animals.

"What's happening?" Nathan asked.

"I'm not sure, but I think Batcat has become a father," his mother said.

CHAPTER SIX

"Batcat!" Nathan yelled out. "Dinnertime!"

The cat came walking toward him on the top of the fence. A row of five squirrels hopped along behind him. Nathan was happy to see five squirrels but worried about the two who weren't there.

"They say that seeing is believing," his father said. "But I've been seeing it for four weeks, and I still don't believe it."

Since the day Batcat saved Munchie, each of the squirrels had decided, one by one, that Batcat was its parent. They rubbed up against him, followed him around and climbed all over him when he lay down. It was all pretty amazing. The big old tomcat with the bent tail and the missing part on one ear had decided he was the mommy or daddy to a bunch of squirrels.

Nathan put down a bowl for the cat, filled with scraps of meat from their meal. Then he put down a plate of nuts and seeds for the squirrels. All six animals came onto the porch and started eating.

Nathan's mother pulled out her phone and started to take pictures.

"You have hundreds of pictures and dozens of videos already," his father said.

"I know, I know, but it's like you said, it's so hard to believe that I want proof after it's over."

"Hello, Munchie, Scruffy, Fluffy, Rocky and Patches," Nathan said.

"I still don't know how you can tell them apart so easily," his father said.

"I'm still not sure why you *can't*. I guess I'm lucky I'm your only child, or you'd get me confused with the others," Nathan joked.

"Kids are a little different than squirrels."

"Not if you're a squirrel...or Batcat. I wonder where Shiny and Bushy are?" Nathan said.

"I'm sure they're not too far away," his father said.

With each day, the squirrels had gotten bigger. And their world had gotten bigger too. Once content to just stay in the backyard, they had now started exploring the whole neighborhood.

"This is the first time they haven't all come home for dinner," Nathan said.

"It's a good sign. They're getting more independent," his mother said.

Nathan reached down and gave Batcat a scratch behind the ears. The cat pressed up against his hand and started with his loud, raspy purring. Nathan had come to realize that the old cat wanted to be pet almost as much as he wanted to be fed.

As the squirrels had begun venturing farther away, it seemed like Batcat was moving in closer. He would come when he was called and had even let Nathan pick him up. Sometimes, if Nathan was sitting on the deck, the cat would jump up onto his lap. Before, there had been days when they didn't see the old cat at all. Now he never seemed too far away and spent most of his time in their backyard or close at hand.

The squirrels' hotel had been moved out of Nathan's room to the backyard. It sat on the corner of the deck. Each night as the sun went down, the seven squirrels would go into the box to sleep. Then Batcat would settle down, snuggled into a blanket placed on top. Nathan knew that with Batcat nearby, the squirrels were safe.

As they sat there watching the animals eat, two more squirrels scurried along the fence. It was Bushy and Shiny. Nathan was relieved that they were all right. Like all good parents, he worried about his children.

"How long do you think it will be?" Nathan asked.

"How long will what be?" his mother asked.

"Before they don't come back at all?"

"I'm not sure, but I know it's part of being a parent. You know that someday your children grow up and go away."

"I'm never going away," Nathan said.

"Yes, you will. To university and then to live in your own home and—"

"I have my own home. This one."

"And it always *will* be your home. But you can't live your whole life in our backyard either. Just promise that when you *do* grow up, you'll come back and visit."

"I'll visit all the time. Do you think the squirrels will visit us sometimes?" Nathan asked.

"I'm sure of it," his father said. "But let's not worry about that. It's just important to enjoy each moment along the way."

The three of them sat back and watched as Batcat and the seven squirrels finished their meal.

CHAPTER SEVEN

Nathan walked out of the house and onto the back deck. After having spent most of the summer outdoors, it was hard to spend today, the first day of school, inside. It was good to be home.

He heard the screen door open and close. His mother appeared beside him.

"I don't see any of them," Nathan said.

"I saw a couple of squirrels this morning," she said.

"Who was it?"

"They were at the far end of the yard, and you know I've never been able to tell them apart that well. It could have been other squirrels altogether."

She knew he was disappointed.

"It could have been Munchie," she said.

"I just hope they're all fine."

Over the last few weeks of the summer, the squirrels had been around less and less. And when they did come, they were more nervous around Nathan and his parents. They didn't climb onto him anymore or even take food from his hands.

Then, one by one, they stopped coming for dinner and to sleep in their nest.

First Scruffy stopped coming around altogether, then Fluffy. Rocky, Patches, Shiny and Bushy followed soon after. That left only Munchie. The first to come and the last to leave. Nathan's father had told him that squirrels were territorial and that they all lived in their own area. Nathan hoped their yard was going to be Munchie's territory.

"I know it's sad that they're gone," Nathan's mother said. "But you have to be happy that—"

"—we had them," he said. "I know, I know. I am happy."

Nathan heard the screen door open again and turned to see his father. He was home from work early.

"How are my two very favorite people doing on their first day of school?" he asked.

"I had a good day," Nathan's mother said. "I have a wonderful class. I'm going to enjoy teaching them this year."

"And you?" he asked Nathan.

"School was good."

"It doesn't sound like it was good."

Nathan shrugged.

"I don't think it's the school as much as the squirrels," his mother said.

"I feel a little sad about that myself," his father said.

Just then there was movement in the yard. It was Batcat. He'd jumped onto the fence and started walking toward them. For an instant they all waited, hoping the cat would be followed by seven little squirrels the way he used to be. There were none.

"It's good to see Batcat," his father said.

It was. The sight of the old cat walking toward them helped to drive away some of the sadness.

Batcat jumped down off the fence and onto the deck. He rubbed up against Nathan's mother, then his father and then Nathan. He even let Nathan scoop him up into a hug.

"I think somebody is hungry," his father said. "How about if we give Batcat his dinner?"

"I'll go in and get it," Nathan said.

"Actually," his mother said, "your father and I were talking about it, and we think we should all go in and get his dinner."

"All three of us?" Nathan asked.

"No, all four of us," his mother said.

"Four? You mean...Batcat?"

"We were thinking that maybe he could eat his meals inside," she said.

"And if he wanted, he could even sleep inside," his father added.

"So he'd be like my cat?" Nathan asked.

"He'd be your cat. Your pet," his mother said.

"That's incredible!" Nathan hesitated. "Do you think he'll come into the house?" Nathan gently put Batcat down.

"There's only one way to find out," his mother said.

"We'll go inside first," his father said. "We'll leave you and Batcat alone."

Nathan's parents went into the house. It was now just him and the cat.

"I guess you heard them," Nathan said. "Do you think you want to be part of our family?"

Batcat rubbed up against Nathan's leg in response.

"You'll still be able to go outside all the time," he said to the cat. "You'll be able to come inside to eat and even sleep inside...that is, if you want."

The cat continued to rub against him.

"I wish you could talk," Nathan said. "I guess there's only one way to find out if you want to be with us."

Nathan walked over to the back door and pulled it open. Batcat looked at him. He tilted his head to the side like he was trying to make sense of what was being asked.

"Come on, boy, it's time for supper," Nathan said.

Slowly Batcat came to the door. He stopped at the threshold and looked inside. He smelled inside.

Nathan bent down. "It's okay even if you don't want to come inside. You're still my cat...or maybe I'm still your boy."

Batcat rubbed up against Nathan. He purred that raspy, loud purr. And then he stepped into the house. Batcat was home.

AUTHOR'S NOTE

When I was about eight years old, my father and I found a starving baby squirrel at our back door. We eventually found seven squirrels, abandoned and orphaned when their mother was killed by a car. Helped by our beaten-up old tomcat named Batcat, we raised the litter until the squirrels were able to be independent. This story, as you can imagine, is near and dear to my heart.

ERIC WALTERS is the author of over 100 novels and picture books. They have won more than 140 awards in Canada and internationally and have been translated into 13 languages. Along with his wife, Anita, they are the Canadian partners in The Creation of Hope (www.creationofhope.com), which provides for orphans in Kenya.

Also by
ERIC WALTERS

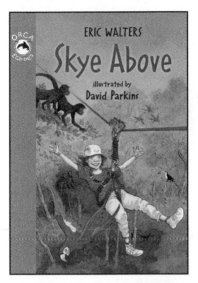

9781459807013 • $6.95 PB • Ages 7–9
9781459807020 (pdf) • 9781459807037 (epub)

CAN SKYE FLY?
SHE'S ABOUT TO FIND OUT.

"Skye's love and experience of animals throughout the book will appeal to readers who enjoy an animal story, as well as readers who enjoy adventure." —CM *Magazine*

ORCA BOOK PUBLISHERS
www.orcabook.com • 1-800-210-5277

Chapter One

Skye looked out the window of the plane. The clouds were thin and wispy. Below, she could just make out the green rainforest and brown fields. Little towns were visible, joined by black ribbons of roads. The horizon blended with the blue of the ocean. Skye had looked out the window the entire flight. She always did. She loved flying. Loved seeing the changing sky. Even when it was full of clouds, there were so many different types to look at.

Her father sat next to her, watching a movie. Skye had never understood why anybody would rather look at a screen than out the window. You could watch a movie in your living room. Of course, maybe her father had an excuse. He was a pilot and flew all the time. Her little porthole wasn't much compared to the big cockpit windows he usually looked through.

A dinging sound announced that somebody was going to come on the PA. Skye knew who she wanted it to be.

"Good afternoon, this is your captain."

Skye smiled. Her father gave her hand a little squeeze.

"We will be starting our descent into Costa Rica. I hope you have all enjoyed your flight. It's a beautiful day, and we have a perfect *Skye* above."

Skye laughed out loud.

"Your mother is talking about you again," her father said. "Although I'm sure you're not *completely* perfect...especially when it comes to cleaning your room."

"I cleaned it before we left," Skye said. Her closet, on the other hand, was a different thing completely.

Skye's mother, like her father, was a pilot. It was on a flight that her parents had first met. It was also on a flight that they had gotten engaged.

They had flown around the world together. And that's why they knew that when they had a baby, they would name her Skye.

Flying had been part of Skye's life since before she could remember. She traveled with her parents often. Everybody assumed that because both of her parents were pilots, her name was Skye, and she loved to fly, she would someday become a pilot too. Skye thought being a pilot would be great, but what she *really* wanted to be when she grew up was a bird.

Of course, she knew that she couldn't ever *really* be a bird. She'd learned that the hard way when she was five and jumped off the roof of their garage. She had flapped her "wings" as hard as she could. Not only did she not lift off, she didn't even slow down. At least, not until she hit the ground. Her mother told her she was lucky she hadn't broken a leg and made her promise that she wouldn't do it again.

Since she couldn't become a bird, Skye surrounded herself with them instead. Her room was filled with pictures of birds. Her bedspread was covered in birds. She had books about birds. She had little stuffed animal birds. Her family hung bird feeders outside the kitchen window. She had a tree house in the backyard that she called her "nest." Sitting up there, she would sometimes be surrounded by birds that perched on the branches. Best of all, she had two canaries—Zig and Zag—who lived in a big cage in the corner of her room.

Zig and Zag loved to sing and would often wake her up in the morning with their melodies. When she closed the door to her room, they were allowed to fly all around. She liked to pretend that she, too, was a canary. She loved having them as pets, but sometimes she felt bad that Zig and Zag weren't free to fly wherever they liked.

The plane touched down. The landing was so gentle that it felt like the wheels just kissed the runway. People in the plane started to clap. Skye was proud of her mother and clapped along with the rest of the passengers.